Dear Panda

Miriam Latimer

Owl
kids

Dedicated to the real Flo and Bea. xx

Text and illustrations © 2013 Miriam Latimer

Published in North America in 2014 by Owlkids Books Inc.

First published by Random House Children's Books, a division of The Random House Group Ltd

Owlkids Books acknowledges the financial support of the Canada Council for the Arts, the Ontario Arts Council, the Government of Canada through the Canada Book Fund (CBF) and the Government of Ontario through the Ontario Media Development Corporation's Book Initiative for our publishing activities.

Published in Canada by
Owlkids Books Inc.
10 Lower Spadina Avenue
Toronto, ON M5V 2Z2

Published in the United States by
Owlkids Books Inc.
1700 Fourth Street
Berkeley, CA 94710

Library and Archives Canada Cataloguing in Publication

Latimer, Miriam, author, illustrator
        Dear panda / Miriam Latimer.

ISBN 978-1-77147-078-0 (bound)

        I. Title.

PZ7.L35Dea 2014   j823'.92   C2014-900169-X

Library of Congress Control Number: 2014931867

Manufactured in Dongguan, China, in March 2014, by Toppan Leefung Packaging & Printing (Dongguan) Co., Ltd.
Job #00198651

A   B   C   D   E   F

OWL kids   Publisher of Chirp, chickaDEE and OWL
           www.owlkidsbooks.com

Florence had just moved. She liked her new room, and her new garden, and most of all, Florence liked that her new house was right next to a zoo.

Florence loved seeing all the animals, but the one she liked best was the panda.

But then Florence had a brilliant idea!

She ran to get some paper and a pencil, and she started to write a letter.

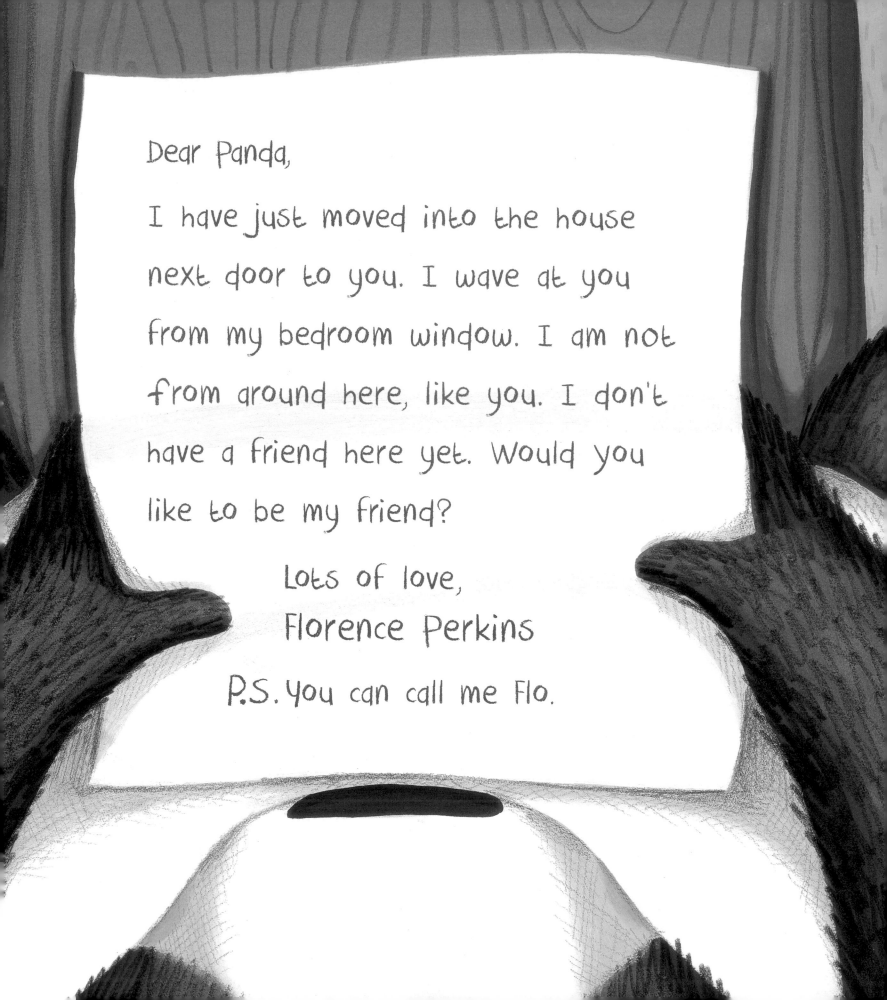

Dear Panda,

I have just moved into the house next door to you. I wave at you from my bedroom window. I am not from around here, like you. I don't have a friend here yet. Would you like to be my friend?

Lots of love,
Florence Perkins

P.S. You can call me Flo.

Panda was flabbergasted to receive his first-ever letter. He pondered, and then he wrote his reply.

Flo jumped up and down with joy when she received the letter addressed to her in the mail.

She tore it open.

So Flo and Panda began
writing back and forth
to each other.

To Panda,
Thank you for the bamboo pencil.
I love it. My favorite food is
toast with jam. Panda, would
you like to come over to my
house to play?
Mom says it's OK.
Bye.

Love, Flo

XO

Panda read his second letter.
He grinned, and then he wrote
his reply.

Dear Flo,
Yes, Please.
love, Panda

WOODSC

So the next day Panda arrived
at Flo's front door.

"Hello, Panda!" said Flo. "I want to
know all about you. Let's go outside
and play together.

"Can you climb like this, Panda?" said Flo.

"I'm OK at climbing," called down Panda.

"And can you swim like me, Panda? Can you?" asked Flo.

"A little," called Panda.

"What about hiding—can you hide as well as this?" said Flo.

"Panda? Panda?
Where are you,
Panda?" called Flo.

"What about hula-hooping?"
asked Flo.

"You are funny," she laughed,
looking over at Panda, who
was a little stuck.

"I am so glad that we are friends, Panda," said Flo.

"Yup," grinned Panda.

"But I'm worried about making friends at my new school. What if none of them are as nice as you, and they don't like climbing or swimming or hiding like us?" Flo said.

"Hmmmm," thought Panda, and he whispered an idea of how he might help.

On Monday morning, it was time for Flo to go to school. The classroom was full of chattering children, and even though her new teacher looked very kind, Flo felt very nervous and alone.

Flo stood in front of the class, and Miss Brook said, "We have a new pupil joining us this year. Meet Florence, class!"

"Hello, Florence!"
the class chorused.

"Florence, can you tell us a little bit about yourself?" said Miss Brook.

"My name is Florence," Flo said quietly, "and my favorite food is toast with jam. I like swimming, climbing, hiding, and playing with my hula-hoop, and ... my best friend is a panda."

The class went quiet. They all stared at Flo. Then they erupted into raucous laughter. "It's true!" Flo nodded. "I've brought him to school to meet you all."

She pointed to the playground and ...

...sure enough, there was Panda, waving at them all.

The class squealed with delight. Miss Brook let them all run outside to meet him.

Everyone thought Panda was wonderful, but soon Miss Brook told them they had to go inside to start their lesson.

As they trailed back in, one girl stayed close to Panda.

"Hullo," smiled Panda.

"Hi, I'm Bea," she gasped.
"Pandas are my favorite!"

"Mine, too!" said Flo,
smiling nervously at Bea.

Panda grinned as Flo and Bea excitedly began to talk about pandas with each other.

"Perhaps we can all play together at recess?" said Flo.

"Yes, please," beamed Bea. "And you can come and sit next to me in class if you like."

"Oh, yes, please," said Flo.
"But what about you, Panda?"

"Time to go home," smiled Panda.

"Oh, no!" Flo sniffed. "I don't want you to go."

"Neither do I," said Bea.

"Perhaps you two can come and visit
me soon?" Panda suggested.

"Yes, yes, of course we will," they nodded together.

Panda walked home, happy that he had been able to help his friend Flo find a friend.

Flo and Bea soon found out that they liked a lot of the same things: swimming,

playing hide-and-seek,

and hula-hooping,

but most of all, they especially liked ...

... PANDAS!